The MANY FACES Of [ERNIE]

written by
from a Sesame Street script written by Judy Freudberg,
Tony Geiss, and Herbert Hartig

illustrated by NORMAND CHARTIER

DISGUISE KIT
Fool Your Friends

This educational book was created in cooperation with the Children's Television Workshop, producers of Sesame Street. Children do not have to watch the television show to benefit from this book. Workshop revenues from this product will be used to help support CTW educational projects.

A SESAME STREET BOOK

Second Printing, 1980